The Porridge
of the
Countess Berthe

To Mina and Clement
and to all Kids of the world
of today and tomorrow

The Porridge *of the* Countess Berthe

by
Alexandre Dumas
Translated by Alix Daniel

First English translation, 2023
By Cybirdy Publishing Company Ltd
101 Camley Street, London NIC 4DU

This book is sold subject to the condition that it shall not, by way of trade, digitalisation or otherwise, be lent, resold, hired out or otherwise circulated without the publisher's prior consent in any form of binding or cover other than that in which it is published and without a similar condition being imposed on the subsequent purchaser.

Translation and Editorial material copyright @Cybirdy Publishing 2023

All rights reserved

The moral right of the translator has been asserted

Original work first published in French in 1845
Hachette, Collection des Grands Romanciers edition 1934

Translated by Alix Daniel

Cover design by Kaarin Wall, illustrations by Eva Vasileva.
Printed by Hobbs the Printers Ltd

This book is typeset in Minion, Proxima Nova and Copperplate
A CIP record for this book is available from the British Library

ISBN: 978-1-7396637-3-5

The Porridge
of the
Countess Berthe

Alexandre Dumas

CYBIRDY
Publishing Limited

London, United Kingdom 2023

Alexandre Dumas is possibly the only writer who has had two bestsellers in the span of one year: *The Three Musketeers* and *The Count of Monte Cristo*, both works of fiction, which are two monuments of universal literature.

Victor Hugo was born in the same year, in 1802, and became a lifelong friend and firm supporter of Alexandre Dumas' writing. Both writers began their careers as playwrights. Alexandre Dumas then moved on to writing travel books from his many travels in Europe, together with pieces of historical serial fiction, which have now been adapted into an estimated 200 films around the world.

Dumas was the son of General Thomas Alexandre Dumas Davy de la Pailleterie, one of the highest-ranking men of African descent from Haiti to lead a French army. Alexandre Dumas wrote *The Count of Monte Cristo*, inspired by his father's story, a story of imprisonment, glory, and betrayal by Napoleon Bonaparte followed by destitution and death in misery. This very story has recently been reignited by Tom Reiss' bestseller, *The Black Count*, which should soon be the subject of a film with the same name.

Though Alexandre Dumas was often mocked for his African descent and frizzy hair, as well as his propensity to create 'commercial literature' with the novel use of ghostwriters (*nègres* in French), he was also beloved and appreciated during his lifetime. He was considered both a great writer and a typical French bon vivant with a taste for the good life and its extravagances. He was known to be a freemason and a member of the Hashish Club alongside Charles Baudelaire, Honoré de Balzac, Gérard de Nerval and Eugène Delacroix. He was once described by the English playwright Watts Philips as "the most generous, large-hearted being in the world."

During his life, Alexandre Dumas built the Château de Monte Cristo at Port-Marly, an eccentric mixture of architectural styles and a beautiful writer's house where he wrote 86 of his novels with the help of his many ghostwriters. The castle was abandoned by its last tenants, The British School, in the 1960s but was later restored with the patronage of King Hassan II of Morocco.

Alexandre Dumas passed away in 1870 due to a heart attack. His death was overshadowed by the Franco-Prussian war and by the denigration of the French establishment of the time.

In 2002, French President Jacques Chirac, in an attempt to

rectify this past discredit, organised a lavish reburial ceremony in the Pantheon, the official tomb of honour, where Alexandre Dumas' friend Victor Hugo and other famous citizens such as Jean Jacques Rousseau, Honoré de Balzac, Pierre and Marie Curie, Aimée Césaire and Jean Moulin have all been buried. The ceremony started in the Château de Monte-Cristo, where writers and artists kept watch over his coffin, covered with blue velvet inscribed with the famous motto "Tous pour un, un pour tous" (all for one, one for all). The coffin was then escorted by the mounted Garde Républicaine and carried to the Pantheon by four men dressed as the Musketeers: D'Artagnan, Porthos, Aramis and Athos.

We are proud to be presenting a 2023 revival of Alexandre Dumas' nearly forgotten novella, *La Bouillie de la Comtesse Berthe*, with this first-ever English translation by Alix Daniel, a French doctor and writer living in the UK.

The Porridge of the Countess Berthe is a goblin tale characterised by Alexandre Dumas' humour and generous-hearted literature. The main character, Countess Berthe, is a medieval noble soul and a kind woman full of ardour, courage and determination. We hope that this translation will help her reach the hall of fame and join many other Alexandre Dumas characters in bringing joy, empathy and interest to the readers of today and tomorrow.

The Beginning

First of all, dear reader, I must tell you that I have travelled the world a little and that, as a traveller, I shall probably write for you a *Robinson*[1] one day, most likely not as good as the one written by Daniel De Foë, but certainly as good as any written since.

So, during one of those thousands of travels I mentioned earlier, I was on a steamer going up the Old Rhine[2], as the Germans call it. I was following not only with my eyes but also with my map and my guidebook on the table. I looked at all the beautiful castles whose time had crumbled into the river, to use an expression belonging to a poet[3] among our friends.

Each castle came before me, telling me about its more or less poetic past, when, to my great astonishment, I spotted one castle whose name was not even on my map. I resorted – as I had already done more than once since Cologne – to a certain Mr Taschenburch, born in 1811[4], the same year as the well-known poor King who never saw his kingdom.

The man I was talking to was not only small, but a good representative of the oblong square[5]. He was full of verse and prose, which he would spout out to anyone who took the trouble to leaf through it.

So, I asked him what this castle was all about. He paused for a moment and replied:

"This is Wittsgaw Castle."

"Can we find out who it belonged to?"

"Certainly. It belonged to the Rosemberg family. Having fallen into ruin around the thirteenth century, it was rebuilt by Count Osmond and Countess Berthe, his wife. This reconstruction led to a rather unusual tradition."

"What is that?"

"Oh, it would not amuse you. It is a child's tale."

"Blast! My dear Mr Taschenburch, you are mistaken. You think your story would not amuse me because it is a child's tale. Well, that is not the case: see."

I pulled a small, beautifully bound volume out of my pocket and showed it to him. It contained *Little Red Riding Hood*, *Donkey Skin* and *The Blue Bird*.

"How about this?" I said.

He replied sternly, "These three tales are quite simply three masterpieces."

"So, do you no longer have any trouble telling me about your story?"

"None, because I can see that it will be addressed to someone worthy of appreciating it."

"But you know that, in a fairy tale, because I presume that your story is a fairy tale, or more or less..."

"Rightly so."

"Well, in a fairy tale, the title has a lot to do with it. Look at the beautiful titles: *Little Red Riding Hood*,

Donkey Skin, *The Blue Bird*…"

"Well, my title is no less interesting."

"What is it?"

"*The Porridge of the Countess Berthe*."

"My dear Mr Taschenburch, my mouth is watering."

"So listen now."

"I am listening."

And so he began:

The Countess Berthe

Once there was a valiant knight named Osmond of Rosemberg, who chose a beautiful young girl named Berthe as his wife.

Berthe could not have competed, I know, with the great ladies of our day, although she was certainly as noble as the noblest. She spoke only good old German, did not sing any Italian, did not read any English, and danced neither the galop[6] nor the two-beat waltz.

On the other hand, she was kind, gentle and compassionate, and took great care not to let a single breath tarnish the mirror of her reputation.

When she travelled through her villages, not in an elegant carriage with a King Charles spaniel[7] on the front seat, but, on foot, with a bag of alms[8] in her hand, a "May God reward you," said in a grateful voice by an old man, widow or orphan, seemed sweeter to her ears than the most melodious ballad by the famous Minnesinger[9], a ballad of note, which was sometimes paid for with a gold coin by those who refused a small copper coin to the poor man standing on the road half-naked, shivering, holding in his hand a hat with a hole in it.

Cobolds

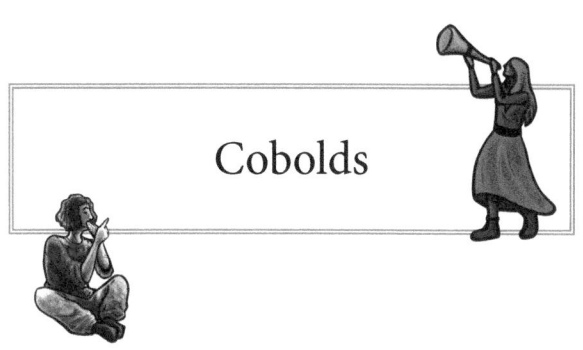

The blessings of the whole region simply fell like a sweet dew of happiness on Berthe and her husband. Golden harvests covered the fields, bunches of huge grapes made the vines crackle, and if a black cloud laden with hail and lightning approached the castle, an invisible breath pushed it towards the dwelling of some wicked lord of the manor, above which it would burst and wreak havoc.

Who was driving the black cloud in this way, and who was keeping Count Osmond and Countess Berthe's estate safe from lightning and hail? I shall tell you.

They were the castle dwarfs.

I must first tell you that in Germany there was once a race of good little spirits, who have unfortunately since disappeared; the tallest of them was barely six inches high. They were called Cobolds.

These good little geniuses, as old as time itself, were especially fond of castles whose owners were, in God's heart, good themselves.

The Cobolds hated the wicked, punishing them with little mischiefs befitting their size, while on the contrary they protected with their power, which extended over all four elements, those who shared their values.

This is the reason why these dwarfs, who from time immemorial inhabited the Castle of Wittsgaw and cared for the fathers, forefathers and ancestors, were particularly fond of Count Osmond and Countess Berthe.

With their breath, the Cobolds pushed the cloud laden with hail and lightning far away from their blessed domain.

The old castle

One day, Berthe entered her husband's quarters and said to him:

"My dear lord, our castle is getting old and threatens to fall into ruin: we can no longer stay safely in this shaky manor. I think, unless you disagree, that we should have another house built."

"I would like nothing better," replied the knight, "but there is one thing that worries me."

"What is it?"

"Even though we have never seen them, there is no reason why you should not have heard of these good Cobolds who live in the foundations of our castle.

"My father had heard it said by his grandfather, who got it from one of his ancestors, that these little spirits were the blessing of the manor; perhaps they have taken up their habits in this old dwelling. If we were to anger them by disturbing them, if they were to abandon us, perhaps our happiness would simply go."

Berthe agreed with these wise words. And then, she and her husband decided to live in the castle as it was, rather than do anything to upset the good little spirits.

The Ambassador

The following night, Countess Berthe and Count Osmond were together in their large four-poster bed supported by four twisted columns, when they heard a sound like that of a multitude of small steps approaching from the drawing-room.

Then, the bedroom door opened. An embassy of the little dwarfs we have just mentioned entered and came towards them.

The ambassador, leading the squad, was richly dressed in the fashion of the time, wearing a fur coat, a velvet leotard, mi-party trousers[10] and small slippers demurely pointed.

At his side was a sword of the finest steel with one single diamond on the hilt. He politely held in his hand his little feathered toque[11,] and, approaching the bed of the couple, who were gazing at him in astonishment, he said:

We have heard the telling
That, in the hope of your prosperous destiny,
A great desire has come to you this evening
To rebuild the castle of your dynasty.
Well done, because the manor is old!
Age has eroded the rocky giant black and mighty,
And water you on rainy days to lead to mould,

Filtered through its mantle of ivy.
Let the old burg[12] roll, knocked down with no value,
And emerge a more beautiful home.
Let ancestors' antique virtue
Come and live in the new home.

Count Osmond was too astonished at what had happened to reply to these words, other than with a friendly gesture of the hand.

The ambassador, however, was content with this gallantry, and withdrew after ceremoniously greeting husband and wife.

The next day, the count and countess woke up feeling very satisfied. The major difficulty had been removed. Consequently, with the consent of his good little friends, Osmond sent for a skilful architect, who the same day condemned the old castle to be demolished and put some of his men to work, while others drew new stones from the quarries and felled the large oaks intended for beams and fir trees for joists.

In less than a month, the old burg was razed to the level of the mountain; and as the new castle, according to the architect himself, would take three years to build, the count and countess decided to retire to a small tenant farm they had in the vicinity of their delightful manor.

Honeyed porridge

The building of the castle was progressing. The masons worked on it during the day, while the little dwarfs worked at night. At first, the workmen were very frightened to find that every morning when they came back to work, the castle had grown a few storeys higher. They told the architect, who told the count, who admitted, although he was not completely sure, that everything led him to believe that it was his little friends the dwarfs who, knowing how much he was in a hurry to get into his manor, were doing this work at night.

One day, a small wheelbarrow, no bigger than a hand, was found on the scaffolding. It was so beautifully made of ebony wood with a silver rim that it looked like a toy made for a prince. The bricklayer who had found the wheelbarrow showed it to his companions, and in the evening wanted to take it home to give it to his little boy.

But, just as he was about to put his hand on it, the wheelbarrow started to roll away on its own and ran out of the door so quickly that, although the poor bricklayer ran after it with all the strength of his legs, it disappeared in a second.

At the same moment, he heard high-pitched, shrill and prolonged peals of laughter; it was the Cobolds laughing at him.

It was fortunate that the little dwarfs had taken on the job, because if they had not done their fair share, the castle would still not have been finished after six years. Indeed, this is what the architect had accounted for, because these honourable stone shifters are usually in the habit of lying by half.

God forbid, my dear reader, you should learn this one day at your own expense!

So, towards the end of the third year, just as the swallows, having taken their leave of our windows and escaping our climates, while the other birds forced to stay in our cold lands became sadder and rarer, the new castle began to take shape, but was still a long way from being finished.

One day, when she was supervising the work of the builders, the Countess Berthe said to the workers in her sweet voice:

"Well, my good labourers, is the work progressing as fast as you can make it go? Winter is knocking at the door, and the count and I are so badly housed in the little cottage that we would like to leave it for the beautiful castle you are building for us. Let's see, my children, will you please hurry up and try to get us there in a month, and I promise, on the day you put the bouquet on the highest tower[14], to treat you with a honeyed porridge, the like of which you will never have eaten before. And what is more, I swear that on the anniversary of this great day, you, your children and your grandchildren,

will receive the same courtesy from me first, then from my children and thereafter from my grandchildren."

In early medieval times, an invitation to eat honeyed porridge was not as small a gift as it may seem at first sight. It was far from being an invitation to be scorned, for it was a way of inviting people to a good, hearty supper. In both cases, honeyed porridge and a hearty supper, dinner was implied, with only one difference: the porridge was eaten at the end of the meal, whereas the soup, on the other hand, was eaten at the beginning.

The workers' mouths watered at this promise. And so they redoubled their efforts and made such rapid progress that the Castle of Wittsgaw was completed on the first of October.

For her part, Countess Berthe, faithful to her promise, had a splendid banquet prepared for all those who had helped, which would be served in the open air because of the number of guests.

However, just as the steaming honeyed porridge was being brought out in fifty huge bowls, thick, icy snowflakes fell on all the dishes.

This incident disrupted the end of the dinner and upset Countess Berthe so much, she decided that, in future, the month of the roses[13] would be chosen to continue this celebration, and that the anniversary of the meal at which the famous honeyed porridge was to be served would be set each following year on the first of May.

In addition, Berthe ensured the foundation of this devoted and solemn custom by a deed in which she obliged herself, her descendants and successors, in whatever capacity the castle came to them, to give honeyed porridge to their vassals on the first of May, declaring that she would not rest in her grave if this solemn institution was not punctually observed.

This deed, written by a notary on parchment, was signed by Berthe, sealed with the count's seal and deposited in the family archives.

The appearance

For twenty years, Berthe herself presided with the same kindness and magnificence over the meal she had founded; but in the twenty-first year, at long last and sadly, she died in an odour of sanctity[15]. She descended into the sepulchre of her ancestors amid the tears of her husband and the sorrows of the whole region.

Two years later, Count Osmond himself, having religiously observed the custom founded by his wife, died in his turn. The family's sole successor was his son, Count Ulrich of Rosemberg, who, inheriting the courage of the Count Osmond and the virtues of Berthe, did nothing to change the lot of the vassals, but did everything he could to improve it.

But then, a great war was declared. Numerous enemy battalions, going up the Rhine, seized the castles built on the banks of the river one by one; they came from the depths of Germany. It was the Emperor who waged war on the Burgraves.

Count Ulrich of Rosemberg was not strong enough to resist. Even though he was an extremely brave knight and would have gladly buried himself under the ruins of his castle, he thought of the misfortunes that this desperate resistance would bring upon the country.

And so, in the interests of his vassals, he withdrew to Alsace, leaving old Fritz, his steward, to look after the estates and lands that were to remain in enemy hands.

Dominik was the name of the General in command of the troops marching to this point; he stayed at the castle, which he found very convenient, and lodged his soldiers in the surrounding area.

This General was a man of low extraction, who had started out as a simple soldier, and whom the prince's favour, much more than his courage and merit, had raised to the rank of General.

I am telling you this, my dear reader, so that you do not think that I am attacking those who go from nothing to something.

On the contrary, I have a great esteem for upstarts when they have deserved the change that has taken place in their destiny. However, there are two kinds of officers of fortune: those who arrive and those who succeed.

Dominik was nothing but a crude and brutal parvenu. Brought up on bread from the army camp and water from the spring, as if to make up for lost time, he had the most delicate dishes and the most sought-after wines served to him with profusion, giving the rest of his meals to his dogs instead of sharing them with those around him.

So, on the very first day of his arrival at the castle, he sent for old Fritz and gave him a list of the taxes he intended to levy on the country, a list so exaggerated that the steward fell at his feet, begging him not to weigh so heavily on the poor peasants. But in response, the General told him that, as the most unpleasant thing in the world for him was to hear people complain, at the first complaint that reached him, he would double his demands.

The General was the strongest, he had the right of victory: old Fritz had to submit.

One can guess that, given Dominik's known character, Fritz was rather badly understood when he came to tell him about Countess Berthe's deed and tradition. The General laughed scornfully and replied that it was the vassals who were meant to feed their lords, not the lords who were meant to feed their vassals; that he was therefore inviting Countess Berthe's regular guests to go and dine wherever they wished on the first of May, and in any case it would not be at his home on that very day.

That solemn day thus passed for the first time in twenty-five years without the happy vassals of the Rosemberg estate enjoying the castle's hospitality. Furthermore, Dominik inspired such great terror that no one dared to ask for anything.

Fritz had carried out the orders he had received, and the peasants had been warned that their new master's intentions were not to follow the old tradition.

As for Dominik, he ate with his usual intemperance and, having retired to his room, posting sentries as usual in the corridors and at the gates of the castle, he went to bed and fell asleep.

However, on that very night and contrary to his routine, the General woke up in the middle of the night; he was so used to sleeping through until dawn that he thought it was the next morning; but he was wrong, it was not yet daylight. Through the opening in the louvre window he could see the stars shining in the sky.

Something extraordinary was happening in his soul; it was like a vague terror, a hunch that something superhuman was about to happen. His favourite dog, which was tied up in the courtyard just below the window, barked sadly. At this plaintive yap, the new owner of the castle felt a cold sweat bead on his forehead. And, at that very moment, midnight began to sound slowly and deafeningly on the castle clock. With each stroke, the terror of the man, who was actually considered by all to be brave, increased so much that at the tenth stroke he could not bear the anguish that had taken hold of him. Raising himself on his elbow, he got ready to open the door and call back the sentry.

But, at the last tintinnabulation, just as his foot was about to touch the parquet, he heard the door.

Despite knowing perfectly well he had closed it before going to bed, the door opened by itself and rolled back on its hinges, as if it had no lock or bolts; then a pale light spread through the room, and the sound of a light step made him shiver to the marrow of his bones. It seemed to be coming towards him.

Then, at the foot of the bed, there appeared a woman wrapped in a large white shroud, holding in one hand one of those copper lamps that are usually lit near a sepulchre, and in the other hand, a written parchment, signed and sealed.

With her eyes fixed, her features motionless and her long hair hanging over her shoulders, she approached slowly. When she was close to the man she had come to find, she brought the lamp nearer the parchment so that all the light shone on it:

"Do as it is written here," she said.

She held the lamp close to the parchment for as long as it took for Dominik's distressed eyes to read the deed that conclusively and clearly confirmed the tradition he had refused to submit to.

When she had finished speaking, the icy ghost disappeared the same way she had come and the door closed behind her, the light disappeared, and the rebel successor to Count Osmond fell back on his bed, where he remained confined until the next morning in an anguish of which he was ashamed, but which he tried in vain to overcome.

Ammunition bread and clear water

With the first rays of daylight, the spell vanished. Dominik jumped out of bed. The more he felt unable to conceal the terror he had experienced, the more furious he became.

He ordered that the sentries who were on guard at midnight in the corridors and at the doors be sent for.

The unfortunate men arrived trembling, for at the moment midnight struck, they had been seized by an invincible sleep, waking up sometime later without being able to calculate how long they had been asleep.

As they met at the gate before the interrogation, they agreed among themselves that they had been on guard; and, as they were perfectly awake when they were relieved of their duty, they hoped that no one had noticed that they had slept and had forgotten discipline.

To all their General's interrogations, they responded that they did not know what woman he was talking about, because they did not see anything out of the ordinary. And so, Fritz, who was present at the interrogation, told Dominik that it could not be a woman but a shadow or even a ghost that had come to visit him, and that this ghost was the Countess Berthe.

Dominik frowned, struck by what the steward was telling him. He pondered silently on what Fritz had previously said to him about the porridge custom, which had been made obligatory by Countess Berthe for her successors and any future owners of the castle, whoever they were, by a deed passed before a notary, and that this deed was in the archives.

After a few minutes of reflection, he ordered Fritz to fetch this famous deed. At first sight, he recognised the parchment that the ghost had shown him.

Until then, Dominik had overlooked this parchment, ignoring it. Indeed, the man was used to knowing with great accuracy the deeds that bound others to him but had very few concerns about those that bound him to others.

Yet as much as the deed was clear cut, and in spite of carefully reading it, and regardless of Fritz's urging him not to dismiss the warning he had received, Dominik decided not to take any notice.

That very day, he summoned his entire staff to a magnificent banquet. It was to be one of the most splendid feasts he had ever given.

The terror that Dominik inspired was so great that, at the appointed hour, although the orders had only been given that morning, the table was set with wonderful sumptuousness.

The most delicate dishes and the most excellent wines from the Rhine, France and Hungary awaited the guests, who sat down at the table praising the magnificence of their General.

However, as Dominik took his seat, he turned pale with anger and violently swore:

"Which moron has put an ammunition loaf next to me?"

Indeed, next to the General was a loaf of bread similar to that distributed to soldiers, like the ones he himself had eaten so much of in his youth.

Everyone looked at each other in astonishment, not comprehending that there could be anyone in the world bold enough to play such a joke on a man as proud, vindictive and hot-headed as the General.

"Come here, dimwit," said the General to the valet behind him, "and take this bread with you..."

The valet obeyed with all the eagerness that fear inspires; but he tried in vain to remove the bread from the table.

"My lord," he said, after some useless effort, "this bread must be nailed to your place setting, for I cannot take it away."

Then the General, whose strength was known to equal that of four men, grabbed the bread with both hands and tried to remove it. He lifted the table with the bread and, after five minutes, he fell back in his chair, exhausted and with sweat on his forehead.

"A drink, scoundrel! A drink, and the best of it!" he said irritably, holding out his glass. "I shall find out, I promise you, who has played this despicable trick: and, rest assured, he will be punished accordingly. So dine, gentlemen, dine; I drink to your good appetite."

And he lifted the glass to his lips; but immediately he spat out what was in his mouth, shouting out:

"Who is the rascal who poured me this repugnant drink?"

"It's me, my lord," said the valet, still holding the bottle in his hand, trembling.

"And what's in the bottle, you wretch?"

"Tokay[16], my lord."

"You are lying, dimwit, because you poured water in my glass."

"The wine must have turned to water when it passed from the bottle into my lord's glass," said the valet, "for I poured some for my lord's two neighbours from the same bottle, and these gentlemen will be able to attest that it is indeed tokay."

The General turned to his two neighbours, who confirmed what the servant had just said.

Then Dominik frowned; he began to realise that the joke was perhaps even more terrible than he had thought at first.

He had thought that the prank had come from the living, whereas in all probability it had come from the dead.

Then, wanting to ascertain the truth for himself, he took the bottle from the servant's hand and poured a glass of tokay for his neighbour. The wine was its usual colour and looked like liquid topaz. Then, from the same bottle, he poured it into his own glass; but as soon as he did, the wine took on the colour, transparency and taste of water.

Dominik smiled bitterly at the double allusion which had just been made to his humble origins, and not wishing to remain near this black bread, which seemed nailed there to humiliate him, he summoned his aide-de-camp, a young man of the top rank of German nobility, to change places with him.

The young man obeyed, and the General went and sat down on the other side of the table.

But Dominik was no happier in his new position than he had been in his old one: under the aide-de-camp's hand, the bread came off the table without difficulty and reverted to ordinary bread, while all the pieces of bread Dominik took were instantly turned into ammunition bread. And, as opposed to the miracle at the marriage feast in Cana, his wine continued to turn into water.

Dominik, impatient, wanted something to eat; he stretched out his arm towards a large skewer of roasted larks; but as he touched it with his hand, the birds grew wings, flew away and fell into the mouths of the peasants who were watching this magnificent meal from afar.

One can judge how astonished they were to see the blessing that had befallen them. Such a miracle was a rare occurrence.

It caused such a stir throughout the world that even today, we say of a man who has wild hopes: "he thinks the larks are going to fall fully roasted into his beak".

But Dominik, who had the honour of giving birth to this adage, was furious.

He conceded that it would be in vain for him to try to fight against a supernatural power, and declared that he was neither hungry nor thirsty, but that he would continue to honour the meal, which despite its splendour, was very gloomy indeed.

The guests were at loss, not knowing really what face to put on.

Then, Dominik announced that he had received a letter from the Emperor ordering him to move his headquarters to another location. He said the request was urgent and so he left on the spot.

I do not need to tell you, my dear reader, that the Emperor's letter was an excuse. What made the illustrious General decamp in such haste was not respect for His Majesty's orders, but the fear, not only of receiving a visit from the Countess Berthe the following night, but also of being condemned to clear water and

ammunition bread for as long as he remained in this cursed castle.

No sooner had he left, the steward found in a cupboard known to be empty until then, a very heavy bag of money with a piece of parchment attached, on which were written these few words:

"For the honeyed porridge."

The old man was very frightened, but recognising the handwriting of the Countess Berthe, he hastened to use this blessed money for the annual dinner, which, having been delayed by a few days this year, had to be all the more sumptuous.

Thereafter, the same tradition happened every single first of May.

The money was always provided by Countess Berthe; until, following the soldiers of the Empire's withdrawal, Waldemar of Rosemberg, Ulrich's son, returned to live in the castle twenty-five years after his father had left.

Waldemar De Rosemberg

Count Waldemar had not inherited the watchful spirit of his ancestors; it is possible that a long exile on foreign soil had embittered his character.

Fortunately, however, he had a wife who corrected, by her gentleness and kindness, her husband's acerbic and biting wit; so that all in all, the poor vassals, desolated by twenty-five years of war, looked upon the return of Count Osmond's grandson as a blessing.

So, the day the vassals looked forward to judge their new masters, the first of May, Countess Wilhelmine persuaded her husband to lead the honeyed porridge party. As she was a charming person and despite Count Waldemar's obnoxious character, everything went smoothly.

Happily, the vassals concluded they had returned to the golden age of Count Osmond and Countess Berthe, an age so often spoken of by their fathers.

The following year, the feast took place as usual, but this time Count Waldemar did not attend, declaring that he considered it unworthy of a gentleman to sit at the same table as his vassals. So it was Wilhelmine alone who did the honours of the honeyed porridge.

One must admit, though, that the absence of the illustrious owner of the castle did not spoil the meal. Indeed, the vassals understood that they owed their happiness to the good heart of the Countess and the influence she had over her husband.

Two or three years passed, during which time the vassals became increasingly aware that it took all of Wilhelmine's pious kindness to soften the angry outbursts of her husband. Her gentleness was constantly extended like a shield between him and his vassals.

However, sadly and unfortunately for them, heaven soon took away their protector.

Wilhelmine died giving birth to a charming little boy called Hermann.

One would have needed a heart of stone not to miss this angel of heaven, whom the inhabitants of the earth had christened Wilhelmine.

For a few days or so, Count Waldemar mourned the worthy companion he had lost.

His heart was not accustomed to tender feelings. So, when he experienced such feelings, he simply did not know how to keep them for long. As a result, after six months, Count Waldemar forgot Wilhelmine and took a second wife.

Who was the victim of this second marriage? Alas! It was poor little Hermann. He had entered life through a door strewn with mourning, and before he knew what a mother was, he could feel that he was an orphan.

His stepmother, recoiling from the care she would have to give to a child who was not her own and who, as the eldest, would inherit the family possessions, placed him in the hands of a careless wet-nurse, who left little Hermann alone for hours on end, crying in his cot, while she went off to dance at fêtes or balls.

The cradle song

On one such evening, unaware how late it was, the wet-nurse was walking in the garden on the gardener's arm, when she suddenly heard the stroke of midnight.

Remembering that she had abandoned little Hermann since seven o'clock, she entered the castle hastily.

Using the darkness to slip away, she crossed the courtyard unseen, reached the staircase and climbed up, looking around her anxiously, muffling the sound of her footsteps and holding her breath, for even though she knew the count did not care and the countess hated the child, her conscience told her that what she was doing at the castle was just dreadful.

She became reassured though, when, as she approached the door of Hermann's room, she could not hear any child's cries.

No doubt the poor child had fallen asleep from crying so much.

The wet-nurse therefore drew the key from her pocket even more calmly, inserted it carefully into the lock, and, turning it as gently as possible, slowly pushed the door open.

But, as the door opened and she gazed into the room, the wicked woman grew paler and started to shake, for what she saw was incomprehensible.

Even though, as I have said, she had the key to her room in her pocket and was quite certain that there was no other key, a woman had entered the room in her absence, and this pale, gloomy and sombre woman was standing by little Hermann, gently moving his cradle, while her marble-white lips issued a song that did not seem to be composed of human words.

Whatever her terror was, the wet-nurse still believed she was dealing with a creature belonging like herself to the race of the living. She took a few steps towards the strange cradle rocker, who seemed not to see her and, still motionless, continued her monotonous and terrible intonation.

"Who are you?" demanded the wet-nurse. "Where do you come from? And how did you manage to get into this apartment, to which I had the key in my pocket?"

The unknown woman solemnly stretched out her arm and replied:

I am one of those people for whom no door is closed
In the grave where for fifty years I have rested
The cries of this child assailed me
I suddenly felt, on my stone bed,
In this extinguished, crumbling corpse,
My heart revive and quiver.

THE PORRIDGE OF THE COUNTESS BERTHE

Poor child brought into this world by a fatal fate,
Whose father is evil and whose mother is dead,
To be handed over to hands that hurt with their touch,
Who can only oppose evil with its weakness,
And fall asleep tonight in his sadness
Like the bird in its song.

Here below, tonight, you will sleep again:
But by the time dawn breaks tomorrow,
Tearing you forever away from this harsh law,

My voice shall descend from the eternal sphere,
A radiant angel will take you under his wing,
And bring you close to me.

And at these words, the ghost of the grandmother, for it was she, leaned over the cradle and kissed her grandson with supreme tenderness. The child had fallen asleep with a smile on his lips and rosy cheeks; but the first rays of the morning, gliding through the stained glass window, found him as pale and cold as a corpse.

The next day, he was lowered into the family vault and buried next to his mother and grandmother.

But rest assured, my dear reader, poor Hermann was not dead.

The next night, the grandmother got up again and, taking him in her arms, carried him to the King of the Cobolds, who was a very brave and learned little genius. He lived in a large cave that extended deep beneath the Rhine, and on the recommendation of Countess Berthe, he took charge of Hermann's education.

Wilbold De Eisenfeld

The stepmother was overjoyed to see the only heir of the Rosemberg family die, but God deceived her in her hopes.

She had neither son nor daughter, and after three years, she herself died.

Waldemar outlived her by another three or four years, when he was killed in a hunt. Some say it was by a boar he had wounded, others say by a peasant he had beaten.

Wittsgaw Castle and the surrounding properties then fell into the possession of a distant relative named Wilbold of Eisenfeld. He was not a bad man. No, he was much worse.

Wilbold of Eisenberg was one of those men who do not care for their souls, who are neither good nor bad, who do good and evil without love or hate, only listening to what they are told, and for whom the last one to speak is always right.

However, brave and valuing bravery, he allowed himself be taken in not only by the appearance of courage, but also by the appearance of wit and virtue.

Baron Wilbold came to live in the castle of Count Osmond and Countess Berthe, bringing with him a charming little baby girl called Hilda.

The current steward's first task was to inform his new lord of the income and charges attached to the property. One of these charges and deeds was the honeyed porridge, which he said, had been respected until then, as far as possible.

So, as the steward told the baron that his predecessors attached great importance to this institution and tradition, and that he himself firmly believed that the Lord's blessing was attached to this custom, Wilbold not only made no comment to the contrary, but also gave orders that every first of May the ceremony should take place with all its ancient solemnity.

Several years went by, and every year the baron produced such copious and good honeyed porridge that the vassals, in favour of this obedience to the commands of Countess Berthe, passed over all his other faults, and his other faults were many.

There was more. Some other lords, either out of kindness or calculation, adopted the custom of Wittsgaw Castle and made porridge of varying degrees of sweetness for their feast days or birthdays.

Among the lords, however, there was one who not only failed to set a good example, but also prevented others from doing so or following suit. This man, who was one of the baron's most intimate friends, one of his most frequent guests and one of his most influential advisers, was the Knight Hans of Warburg.

Knight Hans of Warburg

The Knight Hans of Warburg was, physically, a kind of giant, six feet two inches tall. He was of colossal strength, always armed on one side with a large sword, which he struck against his thigh at every threatening gesture, and on the other side, a dagger which he drew at such moments to accompany his words.

Morally, he was the most cowardly man the world had ever known. When the geese[17] on his estate ran hissing after him, he sprinted away as if it were the devil chasing him.

However, as we have said, not only had Knight Hans not adopted the tradition of the porridge, he also had prevented it from spreading among several of his neighbours over whom he had some influence.

And that was not all. Delighted with his success in this area, he set about trying to get Wilbold to abandon this ancient and respectable practice.

"Good lord!" he said to him. "My dear Wilbold, you must admit that you are very good at spending your money feeding a bunch of idlers who laugh at you even before they have digested the meal you give them."

"My dear Hans," replied Wilbold, "believe it or not, I have thought about what you are saying more than once. Although this meal only comes around once a year, it costs as much as fifty ordinary meals. But, what can I say? It is an institution to which, it is said, the happiness of the burg depends.

"And who tells you this nonsense, my dear Wilbold? Your old steward, is it not he? I understand, as he gets at least ten gold crowns out of his feast, it is in his interest that the feast goes on."

"And then," said the baron, "there's something else too.

"What is that?"

"There are the countess' threats."

"Which countess?"

"The Countess Berthe."

"Do you believe in all those matriarchal tales?"

"Well, they are true, and there are some parchments in the archives..."

"So you are scared of an old, dead woman?

"My dear knight," said the baron, "I am not afraid of any living creature, not of you, nor of any other; but I confess that I am very much afraid of those beings who are neither flesh nor bone, and who take the trouble to leave the other world on purpose to visit us."

Hans burst out laughing.

"So, if you were me," said the baron, "would you not be afraid of anything?

"I fear neither God nor the devil," said Hans, rising to his full height.

"Well then! So be it," said the baron. "At the next

anniversary – and it will not be long, as the first of May arrives in a fortnight, I shall give it a try."

When the baron saw the steward again on first of May, he went back on his original resolution, which had been not to observe the tradition at all, and ordered a very ordinary meal instead of the sumptuous honeyed porridge.

The vassals, on seeing this parsimony to which they were not accustomed, were astonished, but did not complain. They thought that their lord, usually so generous on this occasion had, this year, reasons to be thrifty.

It was not so with the beings who know everything and who presided, as one must believe, over the destinies of the owners of Wittsgaw Castle.

During the night that followed this meagre meal, the Cobolds made such a commotion that no one was able to sleep. Everyone spent the night opening doors and windows to see who was beating at some and knocking at others. But no one saw anything, not even the baron.

My dear reader, the truth is that the baron pulled his bedsheet over his head, as one does when scared, and simply kept still and fully covered in his bed until morning.

Hilda

Wilbold, like all weak characters, could easily be stubborn on certain points. It must be said, he had been encouraged by impunity, for a sleepless night is not such a terrible punishment. And, as he had saved a thousand florins in the process, it was still a good deal.

So, encouraged by Hans' exhortations and not wanting to appear to be destroying such a devoted custom all at once, on the following first of May he summoned the vassals as usual.

But this time, sticking to the terms of the contract which called for porridge, he said nothing about the dinner that preceded it, and requested a pure and simple porridge served without any accompaniment of meat or wine.

Those with a trained palate even noticed that the porridge itself was less sweet than last year. This time, not only had Baron Wilbold done away with all the accessories to the feast, he had also saved on honey.

The spirits of the night immediately became angry. A dreadful row was heard throughout the burg that night, and the next day, tiles, chandeliers and porcelain were all found broken.

The steward made a statement of the damages caused by this accident. It turned out to be as much as the sum that the lords of Wittsgaw would normally spend on their first of May meal.

The steward understood the allusion and did not hesitate to put before the baron's eyes the accounts drawn up and equally balanced.

This time, Wilbold got really angry. Although he had heard the dreadful hullabaloo that had turned the castle upside down for a whole night, he had not yet seen anyone.

He therefore hoped that the countess, who had actually not appeared since the night she had returned to cradle little Hermann, had now been dead too long to leave her tomb.

Since it was necessary for Wilbold to pay a fixed sum each year, he decided to renew the castle furniture rather than feed his vassals.

The following year, therefore, he resolved to give nothing at all, not even the porridge. As he understood that this total infringement of the old tradition would arouse the Countess Berthe to an anger commensurate with the offence, he decided to leave the castle on the twenty-eighth of April and to not return until the fifth of May.

But to this dubious solution he found a sweet opposition.

Fifteen years had passed since Baron Wilbold of Eisenfeld had taken possession of the castle, and during these fifteen years, Hilda, the pretty little child whom we saw there in her cradle, had grown to become more beautiful. She was now a charming young girl: pious, gentle and compassionate. Always confined to her room, she took from her solitary habits a sweet and constant melancholy that went admirably with the look on her face and harmonised wonderfully with her gentle name of Hilda.

Just by seeing her, the most rebellious hearts felt that they might love Hilda one day, while the sensitive ones felt that they already loved her.

Seeing Hilda walking in the garden during the day, or listening to the birdsong which she seemed to understand so well, or at night, sitting by the window, following the moon through the clouds, as if in conversation, she inspired admiration in all who encountered her.

Even when the clouds veiled the moon, Hilda would talk continuously to the celestial body from her windowsill.

So, when Hilda heard that her father had decided to do away with the honeyed porridge this year, she made all possible pleas to him but still within the bounds of filial respect. However, neither her sweet voice nor her gentle looks could melt the baron's heart, which had been hardened by the poor advice of his friend Hans.

On the day he had fixed, Wilbold of Eisenfeld left the castle, telling his steward that this foolish tradition of the Porridge of the Countess Berthe had lasted for too many years, and that, from the first of May this year, he would abolish the custom, which was not only costly, but also was a bad example for others.

Hilda, seeing that she could not change her father's mind, gathered together her small savings, and, as they amounted to the sum that the baron would have had to spend, she set off on foot to the villages that depended on the burg, saying aloud that her father, forced to be absent, would not be able to give the Porridge of the Countess Berthe this year, but had asked her to distribute the sum that the meal cost annually to the poor, the sick and the elderly.

The vassals believed her, or pretended to. And, because the last meal had not left them with very pleasant memories, they were delighted to see a meagre feast turned into a great almsgiving. They all blessed the hand by which it pleased Baron Wilbold to extend his fortune to them.

However, the spirits of the castle could not be deceived and would not be taken in by the pious white lie of the beautiful Hilda.

The hand of fire

On the fifth of May, Wilbold returned to the castle. His first concern was to ask if anything had happened in his absence; but when he learned that everything had been quiet, that his vassals had not complained and that the spirits had not made a tumult, he convinced himself that his persistence had wearied the spirits and that he was rid of them forever.

Consequently, after kissing his daughter goodnight and giving orders for the following day, he went to bed in peace.

But as soon as he was in bed, an uproar started in the castle, a tohubohu the like of which human ears had never heard.

Dogs howled, owls cooed and hooted, cats meowed, while lightning roared.

Inside the castle, chains were dragged, furniture was overturned, stones were rolled.

It was such a noise, such a commotion, such a pandemonium, that it seemed as if all the witches in the region, summoned by the great devil from hell, had changed the usual place for their meeting.

It was as if, instead of gathering as usual at the Brocken[18], the witches were holding their meeting at Wittsgaw Castle.

At midnight, all noises ceased. Then, the deepest silence spread so that everyone could hear the twelve hours ringing out one after the other.

At the last ring, Wilbold, a little reassured, poked his head out from under his blanket and ventured to look around.

Suddenly his hair stood up straight on his head, and cold sweat ran down his face.

For, a hand of fire came out of the wall opposite his bed, and with the tip of its finger, as if with a feather, traced on the dark walls of the room the following words:

To obey Countess Berthe's desire
Baron of Wilbold, God will give you seven days
Or else
You shall see and become the architect of your own demise
Wittsgaw Castle will slip from your grasp
for ever more

The hand disappeared. And then, one after the other, in reverse order to how they had been written, each of the letters faded away.

Finally, with the last letter extinguished, the room,

which for a moment had been illuminated by this quatrain[19] of flame, fell back into the deepest darkness.

The next day, all the baron's servants, from the first to the last, came to ask for their leave, declaring that they no longer wished to remain in the castle.

The baron, who in his heart was as eager to leave as they were, responded with the following: as he did not wish to part with such good servants, he would move to another estate and abandon the Castle of Wittsgaw to the spirits who seemed to claim possession of it.

That same day, despite Hilda's cries, they all left the old burg to go and live in Eisenfeld Castle, which came to the baron from his father's estate and was half a day's journey from Wittsgaw Castle.

Sir Torald

At that time, two pieces of news were causing a lot of gossip and brouhaha in the Rosemberg estate. The first was the departure of Baron Wilbold of Eisenfeld and the second was the arrival of the knight named Sir Torald.

Sir Torald was a handsome young man of between twenty-one and twenty-two years of age, who, although still quite young, had already travelled the main courts of Europe, where he had acquired a great reputation for courage and righteous courtesy.

Indeed, he was one of the most accomplished knights of the time. Marvellous stories were told about his education. It was said that, as a child, he had been entrusted to the King of the Cobolds who, being himself a prince of great learning in all things, had sworn to make him an accomplished lord.

The King of the Cobolds taught Torald to read the most ancient manuscripts, to speak all living and even dead languages, to paint, to play the lute, to sing, to ride a horse, to make weapons and play games.

Then, when he reached the age of eighteen, when the King of the Cobolds saw that he had reached the point of perfection in everything to which he had wished to educate him, the King gave to Torald the following: the famous horse Bucephalus[20], which was known to never tire; Astolphe[21], the famous lance of the knight, which toppled from its pommel all those it touched

with its diamond point; and finally, the famous sword Durandal[22], which shattered like glass the strongest and best-conditioned armour. Then, to these already precious gifts, he added an even more commendable one: a purse in which there always were twenty-five gold crowns.

But almost as soon as Torald had passed through the village of Rosemberg, mounted on his good horse, armed with his good spear and girded with his good sword, he disappeared and no one heard anything more about him.

This mystery only increased curiosity about the knight in the surrounding area.

It was said that in the evening, near Wittsgaw Castle, he had been seen standing up in a boat which, despite the rapid course of the Rhine, stood motionless as if at anchor.

It was also said that he had been seen with a lute in his hand, on the tip of a high rock that rose opposite Hilda's windows, a rock on which until then only hawks and eagles had rested their talons.

But all these tales were only vague rumours, and no one could say for sure that they had met the knight Sir Torald since the day when, armed to the teeth and mounted on his beautiful horse, he had crossed the village of Rosemberg.

The conjurers of the spirits

The hand of fire, as you have seen, my dear readers, had given Baron Wilbold seven days to repent.

However, urged on by the evil advice of Knight Hans of Warburg, the baron decided not to change his mind, and to strengthen his resolve to spend the last three days in parties and orgies[23].

What gave him an excuse, moreover, was the celebration of the anniversary of his daughter's birth, which happened to fall on the eighth of May, as Hilda was born in the month of roses.

Hans of Warburg had fallen very much in love with the beautiful Hilda. Although he was at least forty-five years old, that is, three times her age, he told the baron about his plans for an alliance.

The Baron Wilbold had never really understood all the delicacies of the heart on which young girls usually nourish their dreams of sadness or joy, pain or happiness. He had taken his own wife without loving her.

However, this had not prevented him from being perfectly happy in his marriage, for the countess was a saintly woman. So, he did not think that Hilda needed to adore her husband in order to be happy with him.

Added to these reflections were the great admiration he had for Hans' courage, his accurate knowledge of Hans' fortune, which was at least equal to his own, and finally the habit he had acquired of having as a guest the cheerful and talkative knight, who amused him greatly with his perpetual tales of battles, tournaments and duels in which, of course, he always got the upper hand.

He had neither accepted nor refused the knight's offer, but the baron had let him understand that it would please him if it pleased Hilda, which would probably not be difficult for a brave, gallant and entertaining knight like Hans.

From that moment onwards, the Knight Hans redoubled his care and attention towards the gracious lady of his thoughts. Hilda received all his demonstrations of love with her usual restraint and modesty, as if completely unaware of the purpose for which Hans' attention and compliments were addressed to her.

The fifth day following the appearance of the hand of fire was Hilda's birthday. Keeping with his plans to spend the next three days in celebration, Baron Wilbold invited all his friends to a grand dinner.

As one would expect, he invited his good and inseparable companion, Knight Hans of Warburg.

The guests gathered and passed into the dining room. As each one of them was about to take place at the table, the sound of the horn was heard.

The butler announced that a knight had just appeared at the door of Eisenfeld Castle, asking for hospitality.

"My goodness!" said the baron. "Here is a man with clairvoyance. Go and tell him that he is welcome, and that we are waiting for him to sit down at the table."

Five minutes later, the knight entered.

He was a handsome young man of between twenty-one and twenty-two, with dark hair and blue eyes, who presented himself with an ease which indicated that, during his travels, he had become accustomed to receiving the hospitality of the highest lords.

His sophisticated demeanour immediately struck all the guests, and Baron Wilbold, seeing who he was dealing with, offered him his own seat, as he had done with Hans.

However, the stranger refused the honour. After responding to Baron Wilbold's invitation with a courteous compliment, the knight took one of the secondary seats at the table.

No one knew the knight. Everyone stared at him with intense interest. Hilda alone kept her eyes downcast.

But anyone who had looked at her as the knight appeared in the doorway would have noticed that Hilda was actually blushing.

The banquet was sumptuous and animated; wines were not spared. The noble courtesy of Baron Wilbold and the Knight Hans of Warburg was remarked upon; they gave their best to all.

However, it was impossible for the dinner to pass without some mention of the apparitions at Wittsgaw Castle.

The Knight Hans began to tease the baron about his fear of the apparitions, fear the baron had admitted many times with all the frankness of a brave man.

"My goodness! My dear Sir," said the baron, "I should have liked to have seen you in my place, when that terrible hand of fire was writing on the wall that famous quatrain, not a single syllable of which I have forgotten."

"Illusions!" Hans replied. "Dreams of a stricken mind. I do not believe in ghosts!"

"You do not believe in ghosts, because you have not seen one yet. However, if you did see one, what would you say?"

"I would conjure it," said Hans, banging his huge sword loudly, "for it to never appear in my presence again; I swear to that."

"Well," said Baron Wilbold, "may I make one proposal, Hans?"

"What is it?"

"Conjure the spirit of the Countess Berthe, so that she never returns to Wittsgaw Castle, and ask me whatever you wish."

"Anything I like?"

"Yes!" replied the baron.

"Be careful!" laughed the knight.

"Conjure the Countess Berthe's spirit and ask. Be bold!"

"And if I ask you for something, will you give it to me?"

"Faith of a knight, man of his word."

"Even the hand of the beautiful Hilda?"

"Even my daughter's hand."

"My father!" said the young chatelaine in a lightly reproaching tone.

"My goodness! My dear Hilda," said the baron, slightly intoxicated by a few glasses of Tokay and Braunberger. "My goodness! I said what I said. Knight Hans, I have only one word: conjure up the spirit of the Countess Berthe, and my daughter is yours!"

"And will you give the same reward, my lord," asked the young stranger, "to the one who shall complete the undertaking following Knight Hans' failure?"

"*When* I have failed?" exclaimed Hans. "Are you assuming that I will fail?"

"I do not so suppose, Knight Hans," replied the stranger with a voice so perfectly gentle that it was as if his words had come from a woman's mouth.

"So are you sure, is that what you mean? Zounds, unknown Sir!" said the knight, raising his voice. "Do you know that what you are saying to me is insolent?"

"In any case, my question to the Baron Wilbold of Eisenfeld can in no way prejudice your plans for marriage, my lord, since it is only after you have failed that another will present himself."

"And who is this other who will come forward to accomplish an undertaking where Knight Hans of Warburg will have failed?"

"Me," said the stranger.

"But," said the baron, "for me to accept your offer, courteous as it is, my dear host, I would first have to know who you are."

"I am Sir Torald, my lord," said the young man.

The name had spread throughout the region in such a favourable manner that, at this name, all the guests rose to greet the man who had just made himself known. Even Baron Wilbold did not think twice that he could refrain from paying the young man a courteous compliment.

"My lord," he said, "young as you are, your name is already so advantageously known, that an alliance with you would be an honour for the proudest houses.

"However, I have known Knight Hans of Warburg for twenty years, whereas I have the honour of meeting you for the first time. And in any case, I could only accept the offer you are making me by submitting your proposal to my daughter Hilda for her own approval."

Hilda blushed to the whites of her eyes.

"I have always promised to myself," said Torald, "that I would only take as my wife a woman whose love for me I can be certain of."

Ever since Sir Torald had identified himself, Hans had maintained the deepest silence.

"Well, Sir," said the baron, "since you are submitting the matter for my daughter's approval, and since you are leaving the first attempt of the trial to my friend Hans, I see no reason why, except that I know less about your family, why I should not give you the same word as him."

"My family is on a par with the leading families in Germany, my lord; there is even more to it than that," added Torald with a smile, "and I am going to tell you something you might not suspect, which is that we are somewhat related."

"We are related?" Baron Wilbold exclaimed in astonishment.

"Yes Sir, "replied Torald, "and we shall clarify this later. For the moment, there is only one thing to do, and that is to conjure the spirit of the Countess Berthe."

"Yes," said Wilbold, "I must admit that this is the intention. I am most anxious to see it completed."

"Well then!" said Torald, "let Knight Hans try the test tonight, and I shall try it the following night."

"My goodness," said Wilbold, "that's what I call straight talking! I like it when people conduct their business so directly. Sir Torald, you are a brave young man! Touch my hand[24]."

Wilbold held out his hand to Sir Torald, who shook it and bowed, according the chivalry of the time.

Hans remained silent.

Wilbold turned round and was astonished to see Hans becoming very pale.

"Well, Knight Hans," he said, "here is a proposal designed to please you. Since you were so anxious just now to find yourself face-to-face with the spirits, you must thank Sir Torald for offering you the opportunity to see them this very night."

"Yes, certainly," said the knight, "certainly; but it will be useless and I will have wasted my time. The spirits will not come."

"You are mistaken, Sir Hans," replied Torald, in the tone of a man who is sure of his facts. "They will come."

Hans turned livid.

"Then," said Torald, "if you will give me your turn, Sir Hans, I will gratefully accept, I will extinguish the first fire of the phantoms; probably, they will be less terrible at a second trial than at the first."

"My goodness! Sir," said Hans, "I do not care whether I go first or second. If it is your wish to go first..."

"No, no," exclaimed Wilbold, "I will hold to what we agreed. Keep your ranks, gentlemen. Sir Hans, tonight;

Sir Torald, tomorrow; and so on...."

He filled his glass and raised it.

"Here's to conjuring spirits!" he exclaimed.

Everyone agreed with the baron. But to his great astonishment, the baron noticed that Hans' hand was trembling as he raised his glass to his mouth.

"Fine, then" said Wilbold, "after dinner we shall be off to the castle."

Poor Hans was caught like a mouse in a mousetrap.

At first, when he had agreed to undertake the affair, he thought he could get away with his usual braggadocio. He intended to pretend to enter the castle but spend the night in the vicinity; then, the next day, recount at leisure about the terrible battle he had fought with the spirits.

However, this was no longer possible. As the result of the challenge made by the knight Sir Torald, the affair had taken on a seriousness of character which indicated to Hans that, either by his friend or by his rival, he would no longer be lost to sight.

Indeed, after dinner, Baron Wilbold rose and announced that he was going to accompany Knight Hans himself, and that, in order to avoid any complaints from either him or Sir Torald, he would lock Hans in the bedroom and put his seal on the door.

There was no possibility of retreat. And so, Hans' only

request was that he could go and fetch his armour and helmet, so that he would be in a position to resist the enemy, should the enemy appear. This permission was granted.

Hans went home and armed himself from head to toe. Thereafter they all headed for the deserted castle of Wittsgaw.

The cavalcade consisted of Baron Wilbold of Eisenfeld, Knight Hans, Sir Torald, and three or four other guests who were enjoying the occasion however it unfolded, who would wait the outcome at a farm belonging to Baron Wilbold situated half a league from the castle.

They all arrived in Wittsgaw around nine o'clock in the evening, a good time to start the mission.

Hans was inwardly very worried, but he put on a brave face.

The whole castle was engulfed in deepest darkness, and as the silence was not disturbed by the slightest noise, he seemed and felt like a ghost himself.

They all entered the deserted vestibule and passed through the large rooms hung with dark tapestries and endless corridors.

Finally, the door to the fatal bedroom was opened. Inside it was as cold, quiet and silent as the rest of the castle.

A fire in the chimney was started, the chandelier and

candelabra were all lit. Knight Hans was then wished a good evening.

Baron Wilbold locked the door and sealed it with a strip of paper and two seals bearing his arms.

Everyone then shouted a final goodnight to the prisoner and went off to bed in the farmhouse.

Hans, left alone, first thought of leaving through the window. But there was no way: the window overlooked a precipice that the darkness of the night made seem even deeper.

He then probed the walls. Everywhere the walls sounded back with a dull, muffled sound, indicating that there was no hidden door anywhere.

Whether he liked it or not, he had to stay.

Hans checked that all the pieces of his armour were securely fastened, that his sword was at his side, his dagger correctly drawn from the scabbard and that the visor of his helmet swung freely.

Then, seeing that everything was prepared as well as possible, he sat down in the large armchair opposite the fireplace.

As the hours passed without any sign of the ghosts and spirits, Hans started to feel reassured.

He reasoned that since the wall had no secret door and the main door was closed, it would be as difficult for ghosts to get in as it was for him to get out.

He had heard, though, that ghosts did not bother much with these kinds of barriers. They were known to pass through walls and keyholes with ease and without saying a word.

However, his security precautions provided some comfort for him.

Hans was just starting to fall asleep when he thought he heard a loud noise in the chimney. To his credit, he immediately threw a bundle of wood on the fire, which was beginning to die down, thinking that it would roast the legs of any ghosts that decided to come down this way.

The fire blazed again and rose against the slab, hissing and fizzing. Then Hans saw the end of a plank about a foot wide emerge from the chimney, edging further out without any possibility of knowing who was moving it. The plank continued descending, slowly and at an angle, and when it reached the ground it resembled a sort of bridge over the flames.

Then, on this newly-created bridge, a multitude of little dwarfs began to slide, as if down a rollercoaster. They were led by their King who, armed with all the same pieces as Hans, seemed to be leading them into battle. As they descended, Hans moved backwards in his armchair, which was equipped with small wheels, so that when the King and his army were ranged in battle in front of the fireplace, Hans had reached the other end of the room, prevented by the wall alone from going any further, creating a wide open space between the opponents.

The King of the Dwarfs, after conferring with his generals in a low voice, stepped out into the vacant space on his own.

"Knight Hans," he said in an ironic tone of voice, "I have more than once heard praises about your great courage; it is true that it was always said by yourself; but, as a true knight must not lie, I had to be convinced that you were telling the truth. Consequently, it occurred to me to challenge you to a duel, and, having learned that you had valiantly invited Baron Wilbold to conjure the spirit that haunts his castle, I have permission from this spirit, who is coincidentally an intimate friend of mine, to take her place tonight.

If you are victorious, the spirit, through my voice, will abandon the castle and never appear again; if you are defeated, you will admit with all honesty your defeat and give way to the knight Sir Torald, whom I will no doubt have little difficulty in overcoming, as I have never heard him boasting about having defeated anyone. Consequently, and as I have no doubt that you will accept the challenge, here is my glove[25]."

And at these words, the King of the Dwarfs proudly threw down his gauntlet at the knight's feet.

While the King of the Dwarfs was making his speech in a small, clear voice, Knight Hans had been watching him carefully, and having ascertained that he was no more than six-and-a-half inches high, he began to feel reassured. Such an adversary did not seem to him to be much to fear; Hans therefore picked up the glove with some confidence and put it on the tip of his little finger to examine it.

It was a muskrat-skin armoured glove, onto which small steel scales had been sewn with great skill.

The King of the Dwarfs let Hans examine the glove at his leisure; then, after a moment's silence, said

"Well, knight," he said, "I await your answer. Do you accept or refuse the challenge?"

Knight Hans glanced once more at the champion who was presenting himself to fight him and who did not reach halfway up his leg. Reassured by his small size, he said:

"And what shall we fight with, little man?"

"We shall fight each other with our weapons: you with your sword and me," he said, "with my whip."

"You, with your whip?"

"Yes, it's my ordinary weapon; as I am small, I have to hit from a distance."

Hans burst out laughing. "And you will fight me," he said, "with your whip?"

"I suppose so. Did not you hear me tell you it was my weapon of choice?"

"And you will not use any other?"

"No."

"Are you committed to this?"

"I give you my word."

"So," said Hans, "I accept the fight."

And he in turn threw his gauntlet at the King's feet.

"That is good," said the King, who leapt backwards to avoid being crushed. "Sound the trumpets!"

Instantly, twelve trumpets, mounted on a small stool, sounded a warlike fanfare, during which the King of the Dwarfs was presented with the weapon with which he was to fight.

It was a small whip with a handle made from a single emerald. At the end of this handle were five steel chains three feet long, at the end of which shone diamonds the size of a pea. Apart from the value of the material, the weapon of the King of the Dwarfs was actually very similar to one of those French martinet[26] whips with which clothes are beaten.

On the other side, Knight Hans, full of confidence in his strength, drew his sword.

"Whenever you are ready!" said the King to the Knight.

"As you wish, Sir," said Hans.

Immediately the trumpets sounded an even more warlike tune than the first, and the battle began.

At the first blows he received, the knight realised that

he had been wrong to scorn his opponent's weapon. Despite being covered in his armour, Hans felt the lashes as if he were naked, for wherever the five diamonds struck, they sank into the iron as if it were soft dough.

And so, instead of defending himself, Hans began to scream and shout, running around the room, jumping on the furniture and climbing onto the bed, pursued on all sides by the whip of the implacable King of the Dwarfs, while the warlike tune sounded by the trumpets, so appropriate to the occasion, had changed its measure and character to now become a galop.

It is this same galop, my dear reader, that our great musician Auber[27] found and placed, without saying a word, in the fifth act of *Gustave*[28].

After five minutes of this exercise, Knight Hans fell to his knees and begged for mercy.

The King of the Dwarfs put the French martinet into the hands of his horseman, and took his sceptre:

"Sir Hans," he said, "you are nothing but a woman in reality; so it is not a sword and a dagger that suit you, it is a distaff and a spindle."

And as he said this, he touched the poor knight with his sceptre. Hans felt a great change coming over him; the dwarfs burst out laughing, and everything vanished like a vision.

The Knight and the distaff

Hans looked around; he was now all alone. Then he looked at himself with stupefaction.

He was dressed like an old woman; his breastplate had become a striped fleece petticoat; his helmet, a cornette; his sword, a distaff; and his dagger, a spindle.

You will understand, my dear reader, that as Knight Hans had kept his beard and moustaches under this new costume, his appearance was very ugly and grotesque indeed.

When he saw himself dressed in this way, Hans made a face that made him look even more grotesque.

It occurred to him to undress and get into bed. That way, no trace of what had happened would remain. So he put his distaff on the armchair and set about undoing his cornette. However, the distaff immediately sprang from the armchair where it was placed and gave him such big blows on the fingers that he had no option but to face this new adversary. At first Hans tried to defend himself, but the distaff was so good at it that after a moment Hans was forced to put both hands in his pockets.

Thereafter, the distaff quietly resumed and went back at its place at Knight Hans' side, for a moment of respite.

The knight took the opportunity to examine his enemy.

It was an honest distaff, he thought, like all the distaffs on earth, he presumed, except that it was more elegant than the others and was finished at the top with a small, grimacing, mocking head, which seemed to stick out its tongue at the knight.

Hans pretended to smile at the distaff as he made a move towards the fireplace and, slowly, taking his time, grabbed it by the middle of its body and threw it into the fire.

However, no sooner was the distaff in the fire than all blazing, it burst out and ran after the knight, who this time was not only beaten but also had his skin burnt.

He begged for mercy.

Immediately the flame extinguished and the distaff, modestly and quietly calmed down and took position at his belt.

The situation was serious though.

Daylight was beginning to appear, and Baron Wilbold, Sir Torald and the others would soon be coming back.

Hans pondered and brooded over how he could get rid of the cursed distaff, when the idea occurred to him to throw it out of the window.

While whistling, Hans gently walked towards the window sill. Not to arouse any possible suspicion from the distaff, he opened gently the window as if to breathe the fresh air of the early morning. Then, he seized his enemy and, in one movement, threw it away down the precipice and closed the window.

But then, the knight heard the sound of breaking glass. He turned his gaze towards the second window. The distaff, which had been thrown out of one window, came back in through the other.

This time, having been twice caught out, the distaff became furious and fell on Hans with great blows to the head and bruised the poor knight's whole body. Hans screamed his head off. As he fell back in the chair, the distaff took pity on him and simply returned to his belt.

Then, Hans thought that perhaps he could disarm his enemy's anger by doing something for it.

He set off and started spinning.

The distaff immediately seemed very pleased. Its little head came to life, it blinked with pleasure, and it began to murmur a song of its own.

At that moment, Hans heard a noise of steps in the corridor and wanted to stop spinning, but the distaff did not agree and banged Hans' fingers so hard that Hans had no option but to continue his work.

The steps were getting closer and then stopped at the door. Hans was furious at being caught in such a costume and in such a state of mind, but there was no way around it.

After a moment, indeed, the door opened, and Baron Wilbold, Sir Torald and three or four other people accompanying them all gazed at him, stunned by the strange sight before them.

Hans, whom they had left wearing a knight's armour, was dressed as an old woman with a distaff and a spindle. The new visitors burst out laughing. Sadly, Hans had nowhere to hide.

"Good God!" said Baron Wilbold, "it seems that the spirits who appeared to you have a mischievous sense of humour, Sir Hans. Are you going to tell us what happened to you?"

"Here is what it is," replied Hans, hoping to get away with making a gasconade.

"Here is what it is: it was a bet!"

But at that very moment, the distaff, which understood that Hans was lying, gave him such a violent blow on the nails that Hans let out a scream.

"Cursed distaff!" he murmured, and then resumed: "It was a bet I made, thinking that, as the ghost was a woman, there was no point in waiting for her with any weapons other than a distaff and a spindle..."

At that very moment and despite the pleading look Hans gave to the distaff, the latter rebelled and started hitting him on the nails, in such a way that Wilbold said to him:

"Well, my friend Hans, I see you are lying, and that is the reason why the distaff is beating you. Now, tell us the truth, and the distaff will leave you alone."

And, as if it had understood what the baron had just said, the distaff bowed to him with a nod to signify its agreement.

And so, Hans told what had really happened in every detail. He was willing, from time to time, to deviate from the truth and to embroider some episodes in favour of his courage.

But then the distaff, which kept quiet as long as Hans did not pronounce any lie, fell on him as soon as he did, and in such a way that he was obliged to return to the path of truth at once.

When the whole story was finally told, the distaff made a mocking curtsy to Hans and a perfectly polite bow to the rest of the company, then left through the door, hopping on its tail and taking its spindle which actually followed it like a child follows its mother.

As for Knight Hans, when he was sure that the distaff had gone, he fled through the same door.

Then, amid the jeers of all the rascals[29] who took him for a mask[30], he walked the land to hide in his castle.

The treasure

The following night, it was Sir Torald's turn to keep watch. He prepared for this nocturnal undertaking with as much humility and meditation as Hans had put into it with swagger and lightness.

Like Hans, he was taken to the place and locked up in the chamber, which was subsequently sealed.

Torald did not wish to take any weapons with him, stating that against any spirits, human resistance was useless, because spirits come from God.

So, as soon as he was alone, he devoutly prayed and sat in the armchair waiting for a spirit to appear to him.

He had been waiting for several hours in the same position, his eyes fixed on the door, seeing nothing out of the ordinary. Then, all of a sudden, behind him, he heard a gentle noise and felt someone lightly caressing his shoulder.

He turned round: it was the shadow of the Countess Berthe.

However, far from being frightened, the young man smiled at her as if at an old friend.

"Torald," she said kindly to him, "you have become what I hoped you would be, that is, a good, brave, pious young man; so be rewarded as you deserve."

And at this very moment, beckoning him to follow her, she advanced to the side of the wall which she touched with her finger. The wall opened and revealed a great treasure which Count Osmond had once hidden, at the time he had been forced by the war to leave the castle.

"This treasure is yours, my grandson," said the countess; "And, that it may not be contested from you, none but you may open the wall. The word with which you shall open it is the name of your beloved Hilda."

At these words, the wall closed so tightly that it was impossible to see the seam.

The ghost then gave the knight a last smile and a graceful nod before disappearing like a vanishing and beautiful dew.

The next day, Wilbold and his companions entered the room and found Torald peacefully asleep.

The baron woke the young man, who opened his eyes with a smile. "Friend Torald," said Wilbold, "I had a dream last night."

"Of what?" Torald asked.

"I dreamt that your name was not Torald, but Hermann; that you were Count Osmond's grandson; that you had been thought dead, although you were not, and that your grandmother Berthe had appeared to you last night to reveal a treasure."

Sir Torald understood that this dream was a revelation from heaven and that as a consequence, Baron Wilbold of Eisenfeld would not doubt it.

So, Sir Torald stood up in silence, and courteously inviting the baron to follow him, he stopped in front of the wall.

"Your dream has not deceived you my lord. I am indeed Hermann, the boy they thought dead. My grandmother Berthe did appear to me last night, and discovered the treasure for me; and here is the proof."

At these words, Hermann, for it was indeed the poor child whom Countess Berthe had taken from his tomb and entrusted to the King of the Cobolds, pronounced Hilda's name, and, as the ghost of the Countess Berthe had promised, the wall opened.

Baron Wilbold of Eisenfeld was dazzled by the sight of the treasure, which consisted not only of gold coins, but also of rubies, emeralds and diamonds.

"Come now," he said, "cousin Hermann. I can see that you have spoken the truth. Wittsgaw Castle and my daughter are yours, but on one condition.

"What is it?" asked Hermann anxiously.

"Every first of May, you shall be in charge of giving the Countess Berthe's porridge to the vassals of Rosemberg and the surrounding area."

Eight days later, Hermann of Rosemberg married Hilda of Eisenfeld.

Thereafter and as long as the castle remained standing, his descendants generously and uninterruptedly gave, every first of May, the Countess Berthe's porridge to the inhabitants of Rosemberg and the surrounding area until the end of times.

THE END

Glossary

1. **Robinson:** *Robinson Crusoe* is a novel written by Daniel Defoe (De Föe was the contemporary spelling), first published in 1719. It is generally known as one of the earliest written English novels, launching the start of realistic fiction and becoming a source of inspiration for writers and artists. From its first publication, it became one of the most widely-published books in history.

2. **Old Rhine:** The Rhine became one of the symbols, or a 'memory landscape', of the cultural-historical Romanticism period, with writers such as Lord Byron, the German poet Adelheid von Stolterforth, Mark Twain from America, Victor Hugo, and Alexandre Dumas from France writing exquisite literature inspired by the river and its landscape.

3. **Poet among our friends:** Alexandre Dumas is most certainly referring here to Victor Hugo, his dear friend who, three years previously, in 1842, wrote his only travel book, *The Rhine. Letters to a friend.*

4. **1811:** Napoleon Bonaparte's only son, Napoleon François Charles Joseph, was born in 1811 and was declared the future King of Rome by his father. However, shortly after his son's birth and his defeat at Waterloo, Napoleon had to abdicate and renounce the kingdom of Rome.

5. **Oblong square:** As a Freemason, Alexandre Dumas often referenced Masonry symbols in his writing, such as the oblong square. This particular symbol has been a longstanding puzzle of Masonry symbolism, as the term 'Oblong Square' is itself a contradiction, and because no scholar has thus far managed to trace this phrase's Masonic origin.

6. **Galop:** Named after the horse's fastest gait, the galop is a lively dance introduced in Vienna, Germany, France and England

during the late 1820s. Its origin is possibly Hungarian, and it is unlikely that the galop was danced in early medieval times, as suggested by Alexandre Dumas.

7. **King Charles Spaniel:** King Charles' dog was a spaniel, a fashionable breed in Europe among high society women during Alexandre Dumas' time. A King Charles Spaniel was also called an English Toy Spaniel, originating in England during the 1600s from mixes of small spaniels and Asian Toy breeds. The royal reference was to Charles II, who came to the throne in 1661. Known for his rather wanton lifestyle, the "Merry Monarch" was also a prolific dog breeder, always surrounded by a raft of loving spaniels that followed him everywhere.

8. **Bag of alms:** Also referred to as an *aumoniêre,* a bag of alms was a purse or pouch. It may have originally earned its name from the New Testament's exhortation to provide alms for the poor as part of a Christian's duties. The concept of spontaneous charity was part of life in medieval times, and a Christian of means usually gave money straight from their private purse to a mendicant or a pilgrim. Embroidery bags of alms still exist in a number of collections, such as in the Metropolitan Museum of Art in New York City, the Cluny or Musée Nationale du Moyen Age in Paris, and the Museum für Kunst und Gewerbe in Hamburg.

9. **Minnesinger:** A German poet-musician of the 12th and 13th centuries. The tradition of courtly love songs came to Germany either directly from Provence or through northern France. The minnesingers, like their French counterparts, the troubadours and trouvères, usually composed both words and music and performed their songs in open court so that their art built an immediate relationship with their public.

10. **Mi-party trousers** Popular from the 11th to the 16th century in Europe. The mi-party style of clothing featured two different-coloured fabrics joined together in the middle. Throughout

the 13th and 14th centuries, the style was increasingly worn as many men, particularly vassals, emulated the coats of arms of their feudal lords.

11 **Feathered toque:** This is certainly an anachronism. Feathers were not used as clothing ornaments during the period in which this story is set. According to paintings of the time and historians of fashion, feathers only started being used as an ornament of a toque or hat from the 16th century, at least 300 years later.

12 **Burg:** The Rhine Valley is chock-a-block with burgs built in the early Middle Ages on practically every hillside. They were stone strongholds owned by Burgraves and protected by soldiers.

13 **The bouquet on the highest tower:** Setting up a bouquet on the highest tower could have been a medieval tradition to celebrate the completion of the building of a castle or manor.

14 **Month of roses:** For centuries, the first of May has been a holiday to celebrate spring, renewal and fertility in both pagan and Christian Europe. It is plausible that May could have been referred to by some as the 'month of roses' in the early Middle Ages, the time at which *The Porridge of the Countess Berthe* takes place. Indeed, roses and the culture of beauty attached to them were brought back from the Middle East by the Crusaders, reaching the height of European favour in the 13th and 14th centuries and becoming one of the symbols of the Virgin Mary and the rosary, the most important Christian set of prayers.

Thereafter, the first of May became International Workers' Day, as a result of the infamous 1885 Haymarket revolt in Chicago and the subsequent socialist movement celebrating hope and peace through respect for human work.

15 **Odour of sanctity:** The term "odour of sanctity" appears to have emerged in Christian literature in the Middle Ages, at a time when many saints were raised to that status by acclamation of the faithful. Meaning an actual pleasant olfactory sensation,

odour of sanctity indicated that the individual who possessed it was in a state of grace and never committed any mortal sins.

16 **Tokay:** It is unknown if Tokay wine was drunk in Germany during the early Middle Ages; however, it was certainly a popular wine in Europe during Alexandre Dumas' lifetime. Referred to as "The King of wines, the wine of Kings" by French King Louis XIV, Tokay has not only preserved its golden-sweet perfection over centuries but also its European and Russian reputation as a great and special wine. Catherine the Great, Frederick II of Prussia, Napoleon III, Goethe, Schubert, Beethoven and Liszt, among others, loved it. Queen Victoria was offered Tokaji Aszú every year by Emperor Franz Joseph, and its 2008 limited-edition Essencia decanter was reported as the world's most expensive wine at the time of its launch.

17 **Geese:** In medieval times, geese were seen as heroic figures. A notable story was when Rome was saved from an imminent attack from the Gauls. Geese had cackled and hissed in concert long before the sentries realised anything was happening and, in doing so, saved Rome. Further to their legendary deed, geese had an important part in the manor's court life and subsistence. They lived freely in the castle's inner courts and provided a number of significant products, such as fat, tasty food, feathers for writing materials or fletching arrows, soft down for blankets, pillows and clothes, and wings used for brooms.

18 **Brocken:** The Brocken is the highest of the Harz mountains in North Central Germany, where witches were thought to meet to practice black magic for the sabbath on the Walpurgis night on the first of May. The occurrence of the Brocken spectre, a natural phenomenon of either a magnified shadow of an observer or of a halo-like ring of rainbows, was a source of inspiration for the Romantic movement of the 19th century.

19 **Quatrain:** A stanza or complete poem consisting of four lines. Its form has been used by poets from ancient civilisations in

China, India, Persia, and ancient Greece and Rome, continuing on into the twenty-first century.

20 **Bucephalus:** The notorious favourite horse of Alexander the Great. He accompanied Alexander on many of his campaigns and was renowned for his bravery in battle. Many of Alexander's victories were attributed to the fearlessness and loyalty of Bucephalus in many accounts of his conquests.

21 **Astolphe:** Astolphe, or Astolfo, was one of the twelve paladins of Charlemagne. He was mentioned in the 11th-century French tale *The Song of Roland* as a formidable knight with a magical golden spear.

22 **Durandal:** Also spelt Durendal, Durandal was the sword of Roland, the legendary paladin and imagined officer of Charlemagne glorified in the famous chanson de geste initiating the French medieval epic literature, *The Song of Roland*.

23 **Orgies:** In medieval Germany, there were events where vassals and nobles feasted together with little to no social boundaries. Christian writers and lawmakers reported instances of extraordinary rites, witchcraft, sexual orgies such as in Ancient Rome, and even cannibalism as demoniac costumes. However, the veracity of those written reports is in doubt due to the absence of historical or archaeological proof that such orgies truly took place in pagan medieval Europe.

24 **Touch my hand:** European knights had a clear code of conduct, which addressed not only honour, loyalty, bravery and chivalry, but also the finest rules and codes in gallantry and in verbal or body language with clear codified gestures. "Touch my hand" was always associated with a clear gesture of a hand being offered, and signified "I am willing to trust you; give me your trust in exchange."

25 **Here is my glove:** When a knight said the phrase "Here is my glove", he would throw a glove to the ground in front of his adversary to signify a challenge to engage in combat.

26 **French martinet:** A martinet was a short, multi-tail type of whip made of a wooden handle of about 25cm in length and around ten lashes of equal length, which were used in France as a tool of corporal punishment up until the 1980s. Its use spread from the military realm in the 19th century to whip the dust and mud from coats but also as an instrument of physical punishment in schools, institutions and homes as part of children's corporal punishment. It was named after his creator, Jean Martinet, Louis XIV's inspector general, lieutenant colonel and dreaded drill instructor. He came up with this instrument of torture to replace the classic whip, with the purpose to shorten a soldier's incapacity after a flogging.

27 **Auber:** Daniel Auber was Alexandre Dumas' contemporary, a music composer who became the leading exponent of the French opera *Comique*. *Manon Lescaut*, *Fra Diavolo*, *The Black Domino*, *Gustave III* and *The Bronze Horse* are among the many operas he created with his collaborator librettist Eugène Scribe.

28 **Gustave:** *Gustave III,* or *The Masked Ball*, is a historical opera or 'grand opera' in five acts by Daniel Auber with a libretto by Eugène Scribe.

29 **Rascals:** 'Rascals' comes from the medieval French word, *la rascaile*, referring to the people of the lowest class. Its singular form, a rascal, referred to a low, tricky, dishonest person originating from the rabble or the mob.

30 **Mask:** A mask in medieval times was a person forced to wear a mask in public as a punishment or psychological torture for a dishonourable act. Generally, the mask was used and reserved for the punishment of talkative women whose behaviour had harmed a family's honour. It may have had an enormous nose to indicate the woman wearing it had been nosy or disrespectful. Others had huge eyes, ears or mouths to indicate the crime of the wearer was eavesdropping, spying or spreading gossip.

Love Your Book

The Porridge *of the* Countess Berthe

TIMELINE

NOVEMBER 2023

Soft-back book printed from paper that has been carbon offset through the World Land Trust Scheme.

PRINTED by Hobbs the Printers Ltd
at Southampton, United Kingdom

PUBLISHED by Cybirdy Publishing
London, United Kingdom

SPECIAL EDITION

Cherish your book

WHO are you?	WHO did you obtain the book from?	WHEN did you obtain the book
FIRST GUARDIAN		
SECOND GUARDIAN		
THIRD GUARDIAN		
FOURTH GUARDIAN		
FIFTH GUARDIAN		